THIS BOOK BELONGS TO.

....

....

OH MY GOTH

JOKES FOR WHEN YOU FEEL DEAD INSIDE

OH MY GOTH

Compiled by Andrew Shaffer

LOUISVILLE, KY

Cover design by Andrew Shaffer, using elements licensed from Shutterstock.com. Images on pages 28, 37, 43, and 46 licensed from Shutterstock.

Mass-Market Paperback ISBN: 978-1-949769-47-0

Published by 8th Circle Press (Louisville, KY) / Distributed by Ingram

First Edition

Dedicated to anyone who's ever been told

"It's just a phase."

The world is indeed comic,

but the joke is on mankind.

-- HP Lovecraft

I'm so goth, when I was born, the doctor asked me, "What's with the eyeliner?"

Edgar Allan Poe's parents only let him keep one pet raven at a time.

Nevermore.

I'm so goth, whenever I
knock on somebody's door,
they give me candy.

Q: Why did the goth paint
her nails black?

A: To match her soul.

Q: What’s a goth’s favorite rap song?

A: "Baby Got Bat."

Q: What do you call

a gloomy baby bird?

A: A goth chick.

Q: Why did the broken-hearted poet
cross the road?

A: Because there was heavy traffic.

Only one country singer wears
more black than Johnny Cash:

Goth Brooks.

Q: Where do goths sleep when they go home for the holidays?

A: In despair bedroom.

Q: What did the goth say to the Pillsbury Doughboy?

A: Nice tan, dude.

ABSINTHE

Q: Why did the goth join Crossfit?

A: He wanted to work on his absinthe.

Q: What do you call a goth band
that learns to play their
instruments?

A: Sellouts.

What's that thing called where
your crush likes you back?

Oh, yeah -- a fantasy.

Q: How did the vampire know
he had tuberculosis?

A: He was coffin up blood.

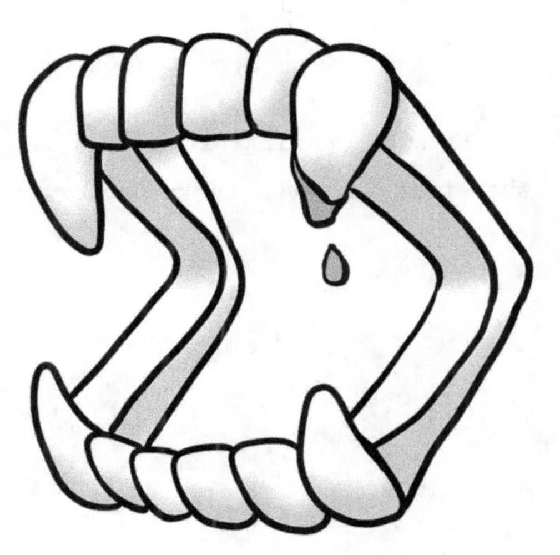

I'll stop wearing black
when they invent a darker color.

Q: Why won't Trent Reznor get into Heaven?

A. Jesus hates nine-inch nails.

Q: What has four legs, a tail, and flies?

A: A dead rat.

You know it's hot out when

goths start wearing purple.

Me: How much for
the goth cucumber?

Clerk: That's a cactus.

Q: Why wasn't the moon hungry?

A: It was full.

Q: What is Debussy doing right now?

A: Decomposing.

Q: What happens if you don't pay your exorcist?

A: You get repossessed.

Q: Why was the serial killer sad?

A: Because he didn't have no body.

Q: Why was the emo girl jealous of her iPhone?

A: Because it died.

You're not a true goth

until you sack Rome.

I'm so goth, when I smile people
ask me what's wrong.

Q: What's the best thing about nihilism?

A: Nothing.

Q: Why didn't Robert Smith get vaccinated?

A: He already had the Cure.

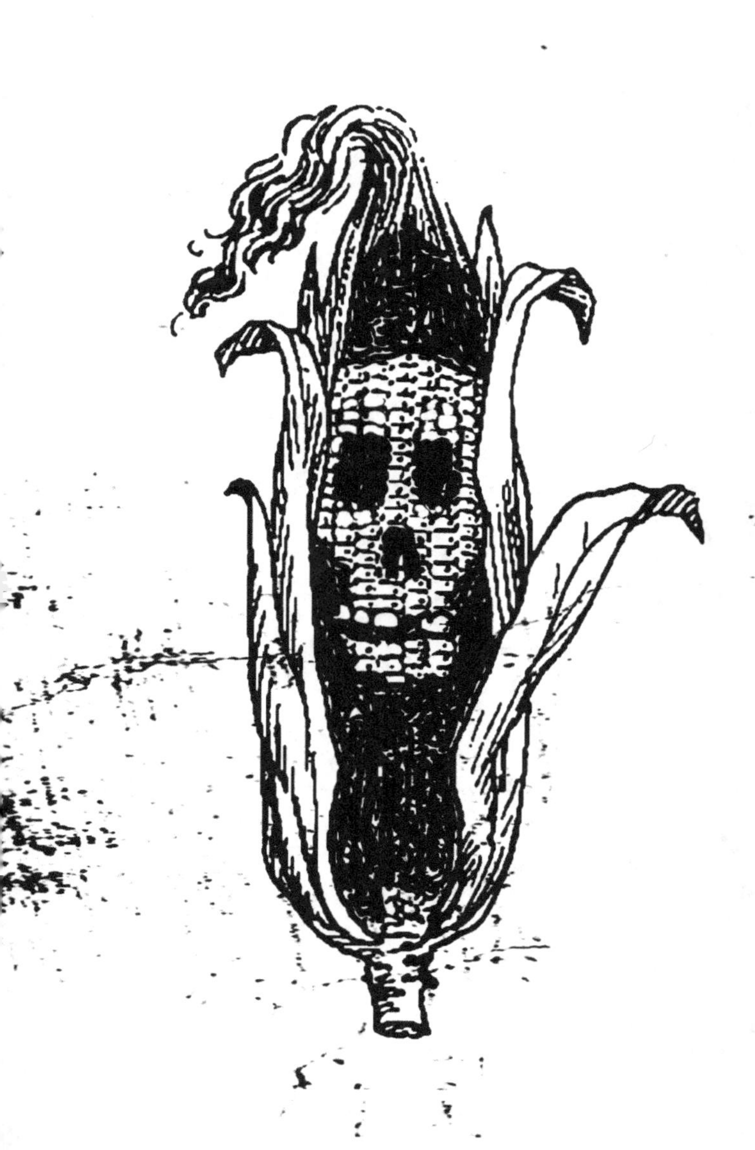

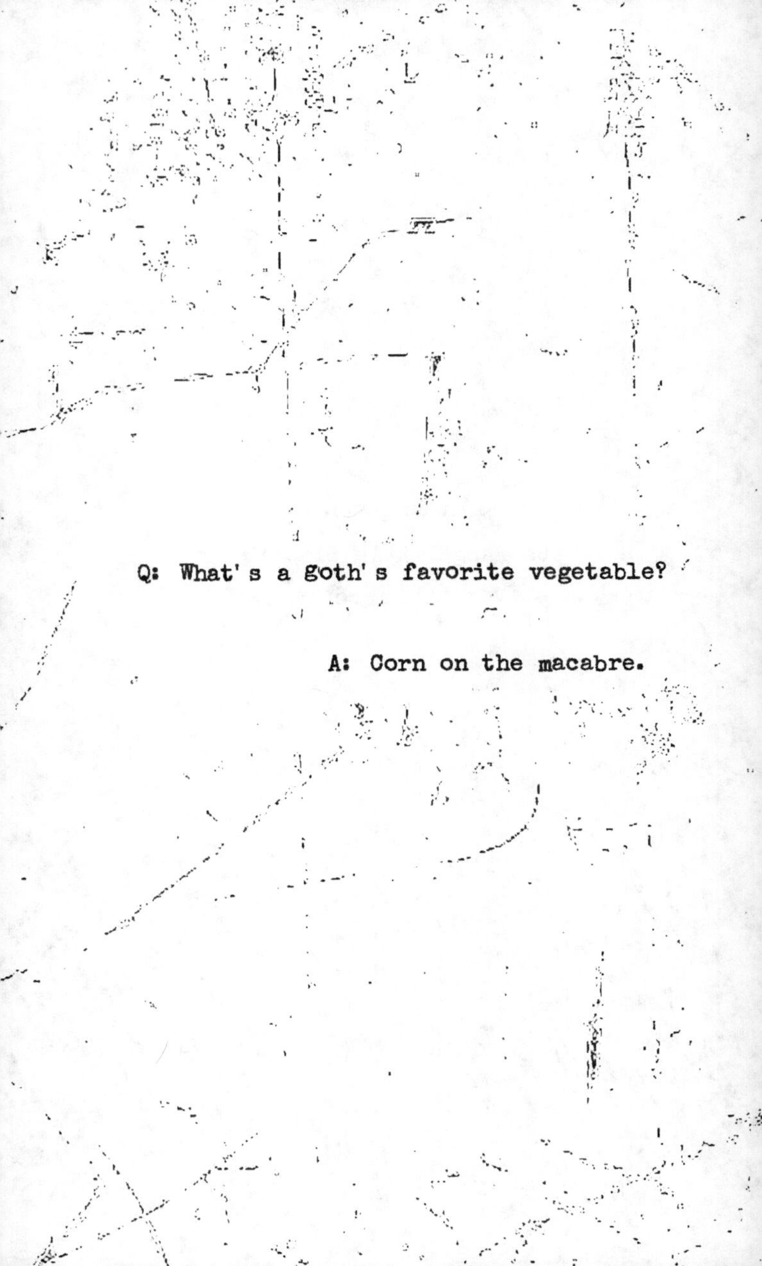

Q: What's a goth's favorite vegetable?

A: Corn on the macabre.

I'm so goth,

bats hang little plastic me's

from their ceilings.

Q: How many emo kids does it take
to change a lightbulb?

A: None, they all sit
in the dark and cry.

Q: Why are there gates around cemeteries?

A: Because everyone's dying to get in.

I'm so goth, I need SPF 30

just to open the fridge.

Normal person: Why do you
always wear black?

Me: Just in case you die.

Say what you want about
Edward Scissorhands,

but I think he's
a pretty sharp guy.

Q: Why did the goth ace
the math test?

A: Because all the questions were
about Joy Division.

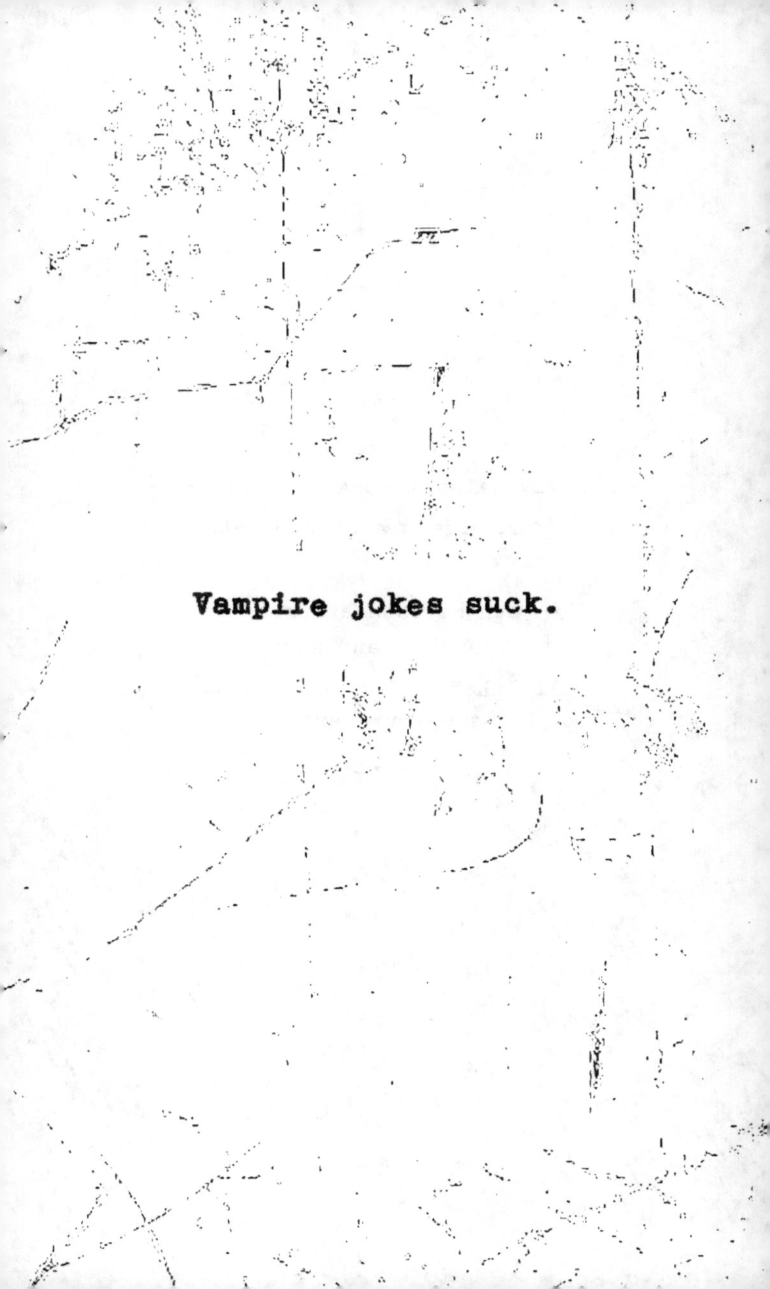

Vampire jokes suck.

A guy walks into a coffeeshop
and orders a dark roast.

A goth barista steps up to
the counter and says,
"If I had a face like yours,
I'd sue your parents."

Q: How do you ground a goth kid?

A: You make him
go outside and play.

Q: Why did the goth leave the bar?

A: It was happy hour.

Q: What did the ghost say when it heard the bad pun?

A: Booooooooooo.

Normal person: Why do you have
a stuffed bat on the wall?

Me: Because there wasn't room
for your head.

I'm so goth, I dyed my shadow black.

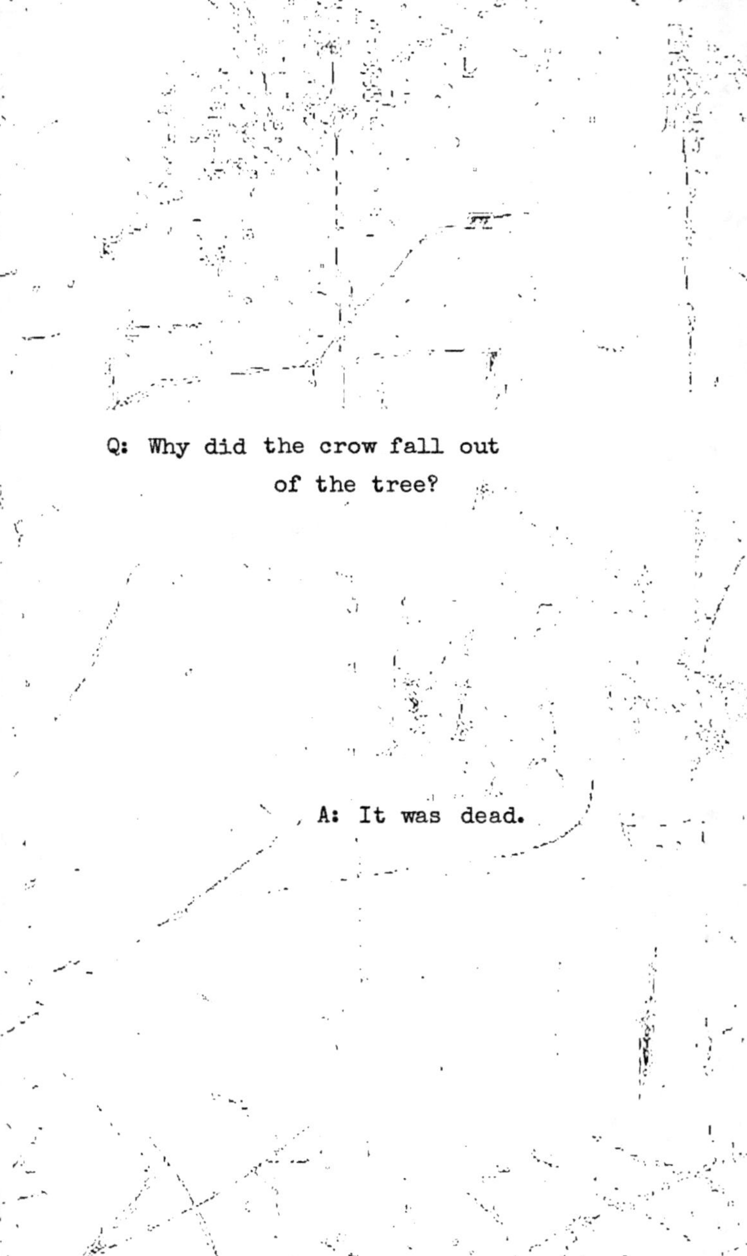

Q: Why did the crow fall out
of the tree?

A: It was dead.

Q: What's the difference between a Tesla and a human skeleton?

A: I don't have a Tesla in my garage.

I'm so goth, I have
a fishnet umbrella.

Q: Where do you find a spider
with no legs?

A: Wherever you left it.

My grief counselor died.

He was so good, I didn't even care.

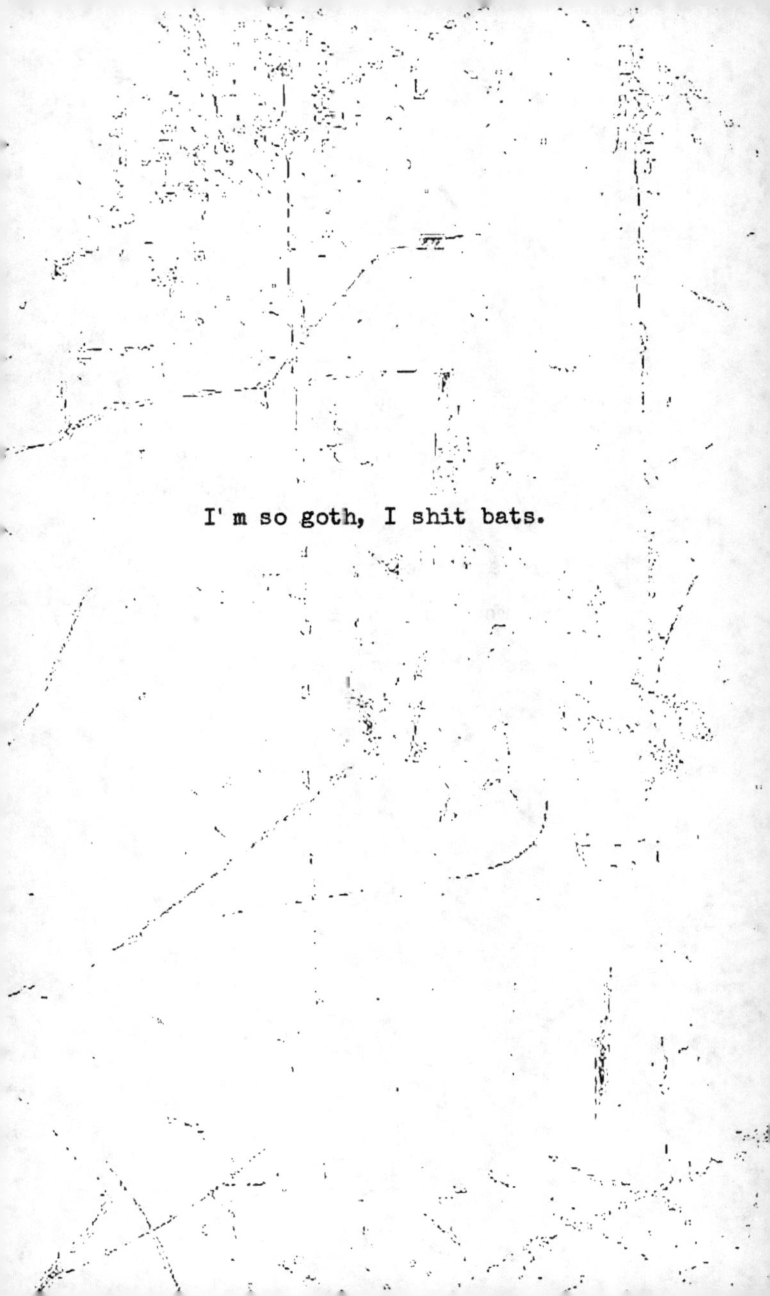

I'm so goth, I shit bats.

There are two types of goths:

Those who shop at Hot Topic . . .

and those who are liars.

HOT TOPIC®

I'm so goth, the dark
is scared of me.

You might be goth
if you go ghost hunting
to make new friends.

Q: What do you call two witches sharing an apartment?

A: Broommates.

I'm so goth, when I sleep
people check my pulse.

Please stop making jokes
about skeletons.

They were once people.
There's nothing humerus about them.

Some people are such treasures
that you just want to bury them.

ABOUT THE COMPILER

Andrew Shaffer is the New York Times bestselling author of the horror novel "Secret Santa." He is a five-time nominee and two-time finalist in the Goodreads Choice Awards.

He lives with his wife, author Tiffany Reisz, and their cats in Louisville, Kentucky.

To contact Andrew or challenge him to a rap battle: www.andrewshaffer.com

LOOK MOM I'M A POET
(AND SO IS MY CAT)
NEW YORK TIMES BESTSELLING HUMORIST
ANDREW SHAFFER
"Always funny." — LitReactor

IT'S BEGINNING TO LOOK A LOT LIKE F*CK THIS

ANDREW SHAFFER

"If you're looking for something tart to cut the holiday sweetness, Shaffer offers a naughty little treat." -- The Gazette

Christmas parodies, essays, poems, and cartoons

www.ingramcontent.com/pod-product-compliance
Lightning Source LLC
Chambersburg PA
CBHW071949190726
48293CB00004B/1410

* 9 7 8 1 9 4 9 7 6 9 4 7 0 *